Incey Wincey Spider

Penny Dann

little ORCHARD

Incey Wincey Spider ...

climbed up the
water spout.

Down came
the rain ...

and washed poor
Incey out!

Out came
the sunshine …

and dried up
all the rain.

So Incey Wincey Spider ...

climbed up the
spout again.